# ANCHOR BOOKS

## *FANTASY AND FABLES*

Edited by

Kelly Deacon

First published in Great Britain in 1999 by
ANCHOR BOOKS
Remus House,
Coltsfoot Drive,
Woodston,
Peterborough, PE2 9JX
Telephone (01733) 898102

All Rights Reserved

*Copyright Contributors 1999*

HB ISBN 1 85930 770 1
SB ISBN 1 85930 775 2

# *FOREWORD*

The challenge was set within these pages to write a story with a beginning, a middle and an end in only fifty words. And so the Mini Saga was born. Lots has been said in very few words, enabling a brief exchange between both reader and writer, yet ultimately creating a stronger bond as characters and stories enfold between the lines. Read on to enjoy the very best in a huge variety of stories, tales, sagas and fables, sure to delight all who read within.

Kelly Deacon
Editor

# CONTENTS

| Title | Author | Page |
|---|---|---|
| Earth Song | Alex Donald | 1 |
| The Attack | Julie Birch | 2 |
| At The End Of A Perfect Day | Marie Housam | 3 |
| Six All The Way | Len Beddow | 4 |
| A Fish Called Spot | Andy Hobbs | 5 |
| An Entirely Different Kind Of Case | Perry McDaid | 6 |
| The Brave Jason And The 'Golden Fleece' | Dimitris Toufexis | 7 |
| Full Circle? | Helen Cullen | 8 |
| Making History | Charlotte Knight | 9 |
| A Paris Rendezvous | Tom Henry | 10 |
| Let Me Tell You This Story It Is About A Man . . . | Joan Smith | 11 |
| Lost On The Moor, Welcomed By An Old Lady . . . | T Hartley | 12 |
| Test For Life | Rebecca Naylor | 13 |
| Hop! | Annie Bethell | 14 |
| A Journey To The Surface | Ashley Cairns | 15 |
| The Story Of A Small English Lady In China | Dorothy Athorn | 16 |
| Dead Roses Bound In Ivy | Cardinal Cox | 17 |
| User Abusers | Jean Paisley | 18 |
| In The Thirteenth Century Whatever Happened . . . | Ann Copland | 19 |
| Uniform | Sally Clark | 20 |
| His Catch | Gemma Freeman | 21 |
| The King | Ruth Walker | 22 |
| Misjudged | Sabeena Jootna | 23 |
| Direction | Jennie McCreight | 24 |
| A Tail Of A Brush With Two Foxes | Jean Eyre | 25 |
| See No Evil | Patricia Whittle | 26 |
| Road Rage | Mick Nash | 27 |
| May Day | Sylvia Scoville | 28 |
| Love's Glorious Triumph! | Alice Blackburn | 29 |

| Title | Author | Page |
|---|---|---|
| Untitled | Hannah Osborn | 30 |
| Untitled | Andrew Gobey | 31 |
| The Art Of Cooking | Paul A'Bear | 32 |
| Encounter | Lorna Jones | 33 |
| The Journey | Emma Hobden | 34 |
| Now I Believe | C Aitken | 35 |
| Stone-Walling | Sheila Bath | 36 |
| Life Can Become Death As Soon As Day . . . | C Lancaster | 37 |
| A Night In The Woods | David Maxfield | 38 |
| The Story Of The Future | Tracey Bratley | 39 |
| The Two Lovers | Andrew Weston | 40 |
| Mystery Date | Charlotte Longden | 41 |
| Untitled | Zoe Porter | 42 |
| Untitled | Rachael Smith | 43 |
| Is He Here Or Is He There? Yeti Could Be Anywhere! | Alan Duncan | 44 |
| Oisin In The Land Of Youth (Tir Na Nog) | Jill McKenna | 45 |
| Campfire Tales | Thomas Harrison | 46 |
| A Journey Through The Galaxy To Earth - . . . | Brenda Casburn-Colvin | 47 |
| The Trip Of A Lifetime | Kirsty Herrin | 48 |
| England Declares War | Teri Backhouse | 49 |
| Great Aunt Emily | H Atkinson | 50 |
| Beauty In The Pool | Carol Wright | 51 |
| One Enchanted Evening | Kathleen Adams | 52 |
| Comprehending Education | K Adlard | 53 |
| The Cage | James Homer | 54 |
| In The Beginning | Katie Whittaker | 55 |
| The Haunting Of Sven The Viking | Sylvia Bangs | 56 |
| Fate Of A Father | Ignas Bednarczyk | 57 |
| School For Murder | Roger Brougham | 58 |
| A Puppet Tied, To A Bloodied, Looped String | Mark Dunn | 59 |
| Narrow Squeak | C Bond | 60 |

| Title | Author | Page |
|---|---|---|
| A Day That He Wished Never Would Have Happened | Samantha Heywood | 61 |
| Clan Of Fallon, Life On The Edge Of Despair | R M Fallon | 62 |
| Willpower | J Craufurd-Stuart | 63 |
| Back In England But What Tension Until You . . . | Phyllis O'Connell | 64 |
| Rules Are Rules | Alfred Smith | 65 |
| Panic | R Prouse | 66 |
| Fear Unsubstantiated | Ivy Allpress | 67 |
| Changing Gear | Vivien Bayley | 68 |
| Sweet Violets | Stephanie Fulfit | 69 |
| Two For The Life Of One An Autobiography . . . | Sue Butcher | 70 |
| Nature's Unnatural | Alexa Marsh | 71 |
| Untitled | Adele Lyth | 72 |
| The Visit | Jean Rhodes | 73 |
| Funfair | Emma Sloan | 74 |
| Our Future | Emma Norris | 75 |
| A Seven-Year-Old's Tale Of Terror | Julia Roe | 76 |
| All Is Vanity | Joyce Brannelly | 77 |
| Sometimes, As We Look Forward, Fate Plays . . . | Wendy Ray | 78 |
| The Sea Can Be Cruel And Unrelenting Yet The . . . | Mary Gardner | 79 |
| The Stone | Brian Parvin | 80 |
| Who Needs Enemies? | Cynthia C Berry | 81 |
| The Drama Saga, Or, It Seemed Like A Good . . . | J Brookes | 82 |
| Box Tunnel | Sallie Chilcott | 83 |
| My One And Only Soulmate | Kerry Ward | 84 |
| The Statuette | Sharon Walker | 85 |
| She Watched The Rides Go Around As He Asked . . . | Claire Hancock | 86 |
| Painful Encounter | Vicky Purnell | 87 |
| On The Floor | William Law | 88 |
| Time Travel | D Falck | 89 |

| Title | Author | Page |
|---|---|---|
| 'Remember When . . . ?' | Joanne Burns | 90 |
| The Stuff Dreams Are Made From | A Doubler | 91 |
| Distopia In 50 Words And A Number | Kay Reynoldson | 92 |
| Holiday Nightmare | Daniel Pillar | 93 |
| A Miracle Is An Unexpected Blessing | Mabel Helen Underwood | 94 |
| Burglar | Jenny Bosworth | 95 |
| Another Night Alone, But Not Alone | Sandra Rose | 96 |
| Till Death Do Us Part | Elsa Wilson | 97 |
| Jack's Mysterious Birthday | Adrian Colley | 98 |
| The Intruder | Heather Henry | 99 |
| I'll Show You, Billy Boy! | Sylvia Bray | 100 |
| The Unseen Enemy | George Woodham | 101 |
| The Ascent - October - 1870 | Alan Titley | 102 |
| The Celebration | Linda Jefferies | 103 |
| To Have And To Hold | J Gray | 104 |
| A Spider's Short Life | D Croasdell | 105 |
| Marathon Man - The Ultimate Challenge . . . | Ella Pearson | 106 |
| Things That Go Bump In The Night! . . . | Amy Law | 107 |
| New Term, New Subject, This Term It's . . . | Richard Farren | 108 |
| Desmond's As Light As A Feather | Adam Gardner | 109 |
| Explosion | Marcella DeSantis | 110 |
| A Living Hell | Angus Brown | 111 |
| On The Train | Vivienne Buckley | 112 |
| The Lady | Jonathon Covington | 113 |
| Soaking Up The Sun On Bikini Atoll | Pat Derbyshire | 114 |
| Were We Dinner? | Holly Langdale | 115 |
| The Alien World! | Felicity Gibbeson | 116 |
| 2034 | James Murray | 117 |
| Talent | Thomas Wignall | 118 |

| | | |
|---|---|---|
| A Personal Story | Bryony Hutchinson | 119 |
| Pursuit | Jonathan Wadsworth | 120 |
| The Polychrome Promise | Susan Devlin | 121 |
| Stalked - The Story Of Mental Torture That . . . | Helen Bancroft | 122 |
| Twelve More Blacked-Out Miles To 23.59 At Camp! | Margaret Clary | 123 |
| Choosing The Future | Charlotte Clark | 124 |
| A Shiny K-night | Paul Warwick | 125 |
| Mysterious Abduction | James Peacock | 126 |
| Shopping Can Be Dangerous! | Chris Jones | 127 |
| The Can Surprise | Martin Karetnyk | 128 |
| Fatal Asthma | Claire Parkinson | 129 |
| Easy Street? | Betty Lightfoot | 130 |
| A Close Save | Jean Anderson Fowler | 131 |
| As It Is On Earth, So It Shall Be In Heaven | B J Harrison | 132 |
| The Mystery Of The East Pole | Michael Childs | 133 |
| Modern Ark | E P Jones | 134 |
| Untitled | Amanda Couch | 135 |
| The Concert | Charlotte McNiven | 136 |
| Grandma's Funeral | Katy Scott-Nelson | 137 |
| My Visit To The Hospital | Katie Jameson | 138 |
| 2023 | Joanne Lax | 139 |
| The Creator Of The Joke Knew; Dinosaura Never . . . | Richard Cluroe | 140 |
| Odin's Children | Frieda Cox | 141 |
| Pipped At The Post | M Williams | 142 |
| Untitled | Susan Hurst | 143 |
| What If It All Went Wrong? | Charlotte Barlow | 144 |
| Heaven Is . . . ? | Pamela Taylor Marshall | 145 |
| The Meeting | Angela Robinson | 146 |
| Let There Be Rain | Claire Harrison | 147 |
| Dusk Encounter | Tim Belton | 148 |
| Untitled | Catherine Spurden | 149 |
| Untitled | Natalie Jeffery | 150 |
| How Lord Russell De Ware Met His Lady | Yvonne E Hicks | 151 |

| | | |
|---|---|---|
| Who Can Foretell What Lurks Malevolently On A . . . | Brigid O'Donnell | 152 |
| Lonely Nights | Michelle Barnes | 153 |
| A Silver Wedding Anniversary | Joan G Brown | 154 |
| My Mate Had Warned Me He Had Neighbours . . . | Chris Creedon | 155 |
| Jecolvic's Fear | Alma Montgomery Frank | 156 |
| Merseyside - December, 1940 | J Robinson | 157 |
| The Interview | Charlena Rooney | 158 |
| It Was Fifty Years Ago Today - Dolly Was . . . | Dorothy Whitehall | 159 |
| Jackpot | Laura Baudoino | 160 |
| The Vagrant | Pat Trixie Ashcroft | 161 |
| What Sights | Keith L Powell | 162 |
| The Journey To Hull | Thomas Woodcock | 163 |
| Badminton | Luke Alker | 164 |
| Cassandra The Sorceress Was Expelled . . . | Anna Bruce Hausrath | 165 |
| Ssh! A Noise? | Heather Edwards | 166 |
| The Last Laugh Of Ellasar Whose Name Means . . . | Maida E Barclay | 167 |
| Archimedes? | Linda Rowley | 168 |
| 50-Word Story | Sharice Barkhordarian | 169 |
| The Past Retrieved | Pauline Phillips | 170 |
| The Great Race | Catherine Sucksmith | 171 |
| The Wrong Van | David Dean | 172 |
| Walking Sixteen Miles At Night Through The Blitz . . . | Susan Roberts | 173 |
| Bandito's Love | Christina Martin | 174 |
| A 20th Century Love Story | Margaret Carl Hibbs | 175 |
| Face To Face | Tony Woods-McLean | 176 |
| Millennium | Norman Royal | 177 |
| Out Of Control | Gillian Snaith | 178 |
| August The Thirtieth, Nineteen Seventy Four | S Mullinger | 179 |
| The Dead Body | Neil Fraser | 180 |
| Family Life | Tom Blair | 181 |
| C And Why | Roger W Chamberlain | 182 |

| | | |
|---|---|---|
| Some Statues Last Forever, But Forget... | Anthony Lascelle | 183 |
| Silver And Blue | J M Stoles | 184 |
| Death Of The American Dream | Keith Tissington | 185 |
| A Packet Of Fags | Barry Flory | 186 |
| £5000 | Fiona Wainwright | 187 |
| Whilst Taking My Morning Stroll On My Favourite... | Janet Rimmer | 188 |
| On The Steps Of The Church | Channon Cornwallis | 189 |

# EARTH SONG

'Push! Push!' they cried.
She screamed. Every year, it seemed, demanded more effort.
The labour pains were intense.
'Push!'
Raindrops formed on her muddied brow. In the warm, damp atmosphere Father Time waited anxiously.
'Push!'
And then the miracle happened.
Spring had come, and Mother Earth watched her offspring blossom.

*Alex Donald*

## THE ATTACK

On entering the alley, a short cut, Mary braced herself.
The footsteps behind her quickened.
When the attack came, she was ready. A quick kick, and her assailant was on the ground, screaming.
'Next time, don't choose a Black Belt in Judo, mate!' hissed Mary as she walked away.

*Julie Birch*

## AT THE END OF A PERFECT DAY

They stood together, after finishing a romantic picnic by the sea.
'Darling,' whispered Valerie, 'you're *so* considerate, starting that new life insurance for us.'
'Naturally.' Roy answered, as he suddenly pushed her over the cliff's edge.
As Valerie hurtled down, she wondered if she'd put enough arsenic in Roy's sandwiches.

*Marie Housam*

## SIX ALL THE WAY

Nervously, Phil tapped the dog hole with his bat, the fast bowler
ran up, delivered the ball with all his strength.
Hissing through the air it came at Phil like a thunderbolt,
he shut his eyes, and swung the bat, a tingle ran up his arm
as he felt it connect.

***Len Beddow***

## A Fish Called Spot

Once upon a time there was a fish called Spot, living in a pond. One day a new fish arrived - her name was Speckle - Spot fell in love with her. Speckle loved Spot too and they decided to live together for the rest of their days, swimming happily ever after.

*Andy Hobbs*

## AN ENTIRELY DIFFERENT KIND OF CASE

Pacing, the man in the deerstalker pondered.
'A sealed room. No-one present but Madame De Range; yet she was murdered under my very nose, inspector - murdered!' The uniformed figures exchanged glances. One nurse whispered to the other 'Poor chap forgot to feed his goldfish again!'

*Perry McDaid*

## THE BRAVE JASON AND THE 'GOLDEN FLEECE'

Jason and his followers arrived at the place.
The dream of getting the 'Golden Fleece' was so close,
but yet so far because of the King.
The Princess fell in love with him and helped him to get it,
but after they got back and married, she killed their children!

*Dimitris Toufexis (14)*

## FULL CIRCLE?

Despite a twenty year age gap - both admitted it was love at first sight!
'Madness' said his friends, he ignored them.
She was his ideal, his soulmate, he was overwhelmed by his need to cherish and protect her.
Untold, thus unaware, that he had once fathered a love child!

*Helen Cullen*

## MAKING HISTORY

The rhythmic hum of the engine evoked his wild tendencies. The intensely passionate inspirations of the crowd burned through his veins. The anticipation of prospective stardom struck him with excessive force. Adrenalin fired. Motor revved. He sailed through the screaming air.
Evil knew he'd exploded into the world's admiration.

***Charlotte Knight (14)***

## A Paris Rendezvous

Standing at the bar, he sweated slightly in the August evening as he finished his cognac. His shrug, in response to the barman's question, was coupled with drooping mouth corners and a glance at his watch.

Turning away, the driver ambled towards the foyer of The Ritz, to meet his passengers.

*Tom Henry*

## LET ME TELL YOU THIS STORY
## IT IS ABOUT A MAN, BORN TO BE KING

A baby was born in a stable, on a cold, starlit night.
Shepherds and kings visited him with many gifts.
As he grew into manhood, he worked miracles.
He healed many sick people, who followed him.
A friend betrayed him.
Beaten and crucified, he died for us.
God's Son.
Jesus Christ.

*Joan Smith*

## LOST ON THE MOOR, WELCOMED BY AN OLD LADY, TELLING TALES BY AN OPEN FIRE

I decided to take a long ride on the moor, with Ali my mare. After a couple of hours, fog came down. Visibility was minimal. Suddenly we saw an old shack, I knocked on the door and old lady let me in. I sheltered by a warm, amber fire.

*T Hartley*

## TEST FOR LIFE

Jimmy had to take the dog for a walk as it was a very special day, he was told. he got onto the field and was dragged away by two men. He pointed to where he thought he heard a buzzing noise coming from,. Wrong. *Bang!* He had failed the test.

***Rebecca Naylor (13)***

## Hop!

He had to reach her before the others. The slick black place lay between them, where the monsters thundered.
But the urge to be with her in the cool waters. Hop . . . there she was, but they were there, handsome, green . . . hop.
No! The bright monster . . .
'Mommy! You squashed the frog!'

*Annie Bethell (15)*

## A JOURNEY TO THE SURFACE

Gliding towards the shimmering light, the young mermaid makes her first journey to the water's face, unable to imagine what the strange creatures who live above must look like, or if they even exist. She rises to the surface and in dismay, realises that all she can see is water.

*Ashley Cairns*

## THE STORY OF A SMALL ENGLISH LADY IN CHINA

To the Lord High Mandarin, rich, powerful, official, but of compassionate nature, came a young, brave, remarkable woman. Detesting the dreadful practice of binding and deforming baby girls' feet, she pleaded to the Mandarin, he agreed to end this cruel habit.

The good lady's name was Chinese missionary, Gladys Alyward.

*Dorothy Athorn*

## DEAD ROSES BOUND IN IVY

Wings at the window. A moth?
He comes with the moonlight, pale in the dark.
Smile melts ice, hand of velvet, kiss of satin.
Candle flickers. Drapes his jacket over the mirror.
In the morning, your lover is gone, with
only a blood stain to say he had ever been.

***Cardinal Cox***

## USER ABUSERS

Crossing the road her foot was an inch from the needle.
It could have jabbed her ankle with what disease, who could tell.
Later, her back door handle was turning as she watched.
Moving her lace, she saw a cat's demented face,
red eyes bulging from fur, noisily clawing glass.

*Jean Paisley*

## IN THE THIRTEENTH CENTURY WHATEVER HAPPENED TO 'ERIC THE RED'? HIS FRIEND MAY BE DEAD!

Huddled by an open fire, sitting with legs crossed on their animal skins which they acquired from hunting with spears. The Vikings began their sea voyages and struggles in the wild for a nice tasty piece of meat. A joint wafting out appetising aromas on a spit-roast!

*Ann Copland*

## UNIFORM

Rows of them, lined up in their identical clothing
waiting for the signal.
It goes, they move unsynchronised and noisy.
They are yet to learn the rules.
'Back!' the official shouts. 'Do it again.'
Their daily routine until they are given permission
to leave at the end of Year Eleven.

*Sally Clark (17)*

## HIS CATCH

He was over the moon, he hadn't pulled in ages.
She was beautiful and just now he liked them smooth and wet.
He told his friends 'Ten pound carp, I reckon lads.'

**Gemma Freeman (17)**

## THE KING

He had a guitar for his birthday, but always preferred to dance.
Everyone mocked him resembling a colourful, crazed cartoon.
He didn't stand a chance in the singing competition -
jerking on tip-toes with hair gelled back.
'Don't be blue, I'll buy you those suede shoes you wanted,'
sympathised mum.

*Ruth Walker (17)*

## MISJUDGED

We all prepare for the melancholy morning of Fred's funeral.
The coffin's lowered. A minute's silence is held in his honour.
'Earth to earth, ashes to ashes, dust to dust' proclaims the vicar.
A cry of desperation comes from below.
'I'm alive, let me out of here.'

**Sabeena Jootna (16)**

## DIRECTION

He was blinded by the light that came from above.
He was told it would lead him in the right path,
it had led everyone else. Yet sometimes the light
wasn't clear enough. He didn't want to lose his life.
If he got to the lighthouse, he'd be safe.

***Jennie McCreight (14)***

## A TAIL OF A BRUSH WITH TWO FOXES

Tom sat on the old bench surveying a good morning's work on the allotment - his pride and joy.
Suddenly two foxes appeared, tearing through his plot - wrecking it in minutes.
Whilst trying to tackle them - one lunged at him.
He awoke to his dog licking his face - his allotment intact.

*Jean Eyre*

## SEE NO EVIL

A tourist in a Moroccan bazaar
Smiled wryly at a notice above
a stall, stating:
You steal! You die!
From the strange objects displayed,
he slyly pocketed an evil looking glass eye,
then left without paying.
He was later found dead, minus one eye,
clasped in his own bloodied fingers!

*Patricia Whittle*

## ROAD RAGE

As I approached a corner, a woman leaned out of the oncoming car and shouted 'Pig!' I leaned out of my window, pleased with my powers of instant repartee, and yelled out, 'Cow!'
I then withdrew my head from my window, drove round the corner, and ran over a pig.

*Mick Nash*

## MAY DAY

At last, her divorce behind her, the house divided into two and Sandra was in love again. Phillip and Tina were teenagers and would soon leave home for university. Her world was good. Arriving at work, she opened her pay packet. She stared. 'From 30.5.99 you are redundant.'

***Sylvia Scoville***

## LOVE'S GLORIOUS TRIUMPH!

Give me Bethlehem's manger,
angels' chorus, Egypt's pyramids,
Nazareth's carpentry and
Palestine's roads.
Heaven's royalty walked here;
ministered, healed, raised the dead,
but ended in disciple's treachery and
> A Cross!

Love's glorious triumph -
> *Resurrection!*

Thankful prayers ascend heavenward!
'I will come again;
be ready!'
Jesus speaks as the *Redeemer* -
> *Resurrected!*

**Alice Blackburn**

## UNTITLED

She had never felt so down,
how could her father do this?
She'd begged and pleaded him to
marry her and he'd refused.
He'd ruined everything, it was her dream,
her wish and he'd refused her.
She tried to forget about it by
busying herself ironing her
father's cassock.

*Hannah Osborn (14)*

## UNTITLED

He savoured the lamb - beautiful,
and so was everything else, a perfect meal.
He would have liked to compliment the chef,
if only there was time . . .
then the cell door swung open and
the priest walked solemnly in.

***Andrew Gobey (14)***

## THE ART OF COOKING

The smell of roasting flesh drew the attention of the hoofed animal away from his current sweat inducing activity. He knew this scent very well, but still could not resist its power. The barbecuing of the damned always brought a smile to Lucifer and warmed his sticky red face.

*Paul A'Bear*

## ENCOUNTER

He drove slowly, edging the kerb. His heart was pounding as he neared the corner. Fumbling with his wallet, he ground to a halt, beside the lady.
'Big Mac and fries, please love' he said.

*Lorna Jones (17)*

# THE JOURNEY

He put on his usual clothes and sat in his open-topped seasonal vehicle. He put his luggage in the back and prepared to travel across the world.
He waved goodbye to his wife, and pulled away leaving a trail of sparkling dust.
'Ho! Ho! Ho!' shouted Santa.

*Emma Hobden*

## NOW I BELIEVE

I took him to his dwelling - just a tramp.
Late at night he returned with thanks.
A ring; was all his worldly goods - from times gone by.
Morning brought a call - they couldn't find the gift
from the dying man. I said 'That's all right
I received it last night.'

*C Aitken*

## STONE-WALLING

The Emperor's reputation was at stake:
He had installed hot and cold baths in the garrisons
but much of the seventy-three miles of frontier road
was crooked, not aesthetically straight. Hardknot Pass
convolutions might deter his horse-powered soldiers.
Then Hadrian smiled. His wall would definitely keep
the Britons out.

*Sheila Bath*

## LIFE CAN BECOME DEATH AS SOON AS DAY CAN BECOME NIGHT

The tall, dark figure emerged as I entered the shop.
Silence! Knife pierces my flesh.
Turmoil! Falling! Confused!
He left as quickly as he came,
Blood seeping, a pool surrounds me.
The weapon was removed, so too was the cash box.
Life was taken, all that is left is *death!*

***C Lancaster***

## A Night In The Woods

When I was a young child, I got lost in the woods.
Luckily I found a cabin, the wind was howling outside.
I heard noises and saw strange things in the darkness.
The door opened slowly with a loud creak,
it was my mum, I was in the shed.

*David Maxfield (13)*

## THE STORY OF THE FUTURE

It is the year 3000. No-one goes outside. They do not need to. all they need is the Internet. The Internet provides a full meal strip of bubblegum and a thirst-quenching crisp out of the modem. This is what it will be like in the year of 3000.

*Tracey Bratley (11)*

## THE TWO LOVERS

His nickname was Tiggy, hers was Ginger.
They did everything together with undying love.
They even went butterfly catching together.
Then one tragic day, Ginger walked in the road and was killed.
They say cats have nine lives. She only had one.

*Andrew Weston (14)*

## Mystery Date

She was getting ready for her date.
It had been a competition in a magazine
entitled 'Win a Mystery Date'.
She had entered and won.
As she got to the cinema she saw her best friend -
a boy, waiting at the meeting place.

***Charlotte Longden***

## Untitled

The nurse looked at the X-rays of the skull,
examining them, pointing to a dark patch,
the doctor was scared, he had to do something.
'Have a specialist look at it?'
'No, I know a procedure' the nurse assured.
'Ready?' She slammed the door,
out came the rotten tooth.

***Zoe Porter (14)***

## UNTITLED

The wind howled outside as it rattled the window pane.
Rain beating on the roof made me uneasy.
The body on the floor and the scissors in my hand.
I suppose I felt bad about what I'd done.
Where would I get another mannequin at this time of night?

***Rachael Smith (14)***

## IS HE HERE OR IS HE THERE?
## YETI COULD BE ANYWHERE!

Two men sought the abominable snowman.
They followed fresh footprints in the snow.
Then, suddenly and too late, they saw it -
a large, brown bear!

*Alan Duncan*

## OISIN IN THE LAND OF YOUTH (TIR NA NOG)

Oisin was homesick and bored. The Land of Youth was just too perfect. He persuaded Niamh to let him go home for a visit. But when he touched Ireland, disaster! He turned into an old, old man - for a day in the Land of Youth is a year everywhere else.

*Jill McKenna*

## CAMPFIRE TALES

Hundreds of years ago, peasants and alike would sit around a campfire listening to crackles and roars of the flames, smoke billowing into the uncharted, star-speckled sky.

Stories of almighty gods, heroic men, battling for our insignificant, yet special lives.

The tale's beginning was easy,
conquest and love.
Finishing . . .

***Thomas Harrison (12)***

## A Journey Through The Galaxy To Earth - Opening The Door To The Future

Year 3008, on planet Venus spacecraft lifts off, destination Earth. On board, holiday aliens landing on Earth shortly, their excited jargon, 'Wonder what Earth's like? Will earthlings embrace us?' Seven days later, back on Venus, ecstatic aliens report 'Earth was everything it's cracked up to be, it's a wondrous place.'

*Brenda Casburn-Colvin*

## THE TRIP OF A LIFETIME

He was so pleased with himself,
and he hoped she would be too.
He couldn't believe how lucky he'd been,
perhaps now his marriage was saved.
He glanced at the tickets in his hand.
Yes, he thought, Titanic is going to solve
all my problems.

***Kirsty Herrin  (13)***

## ENGLAND DECLARES WAR

'Zieg heil' was the cry of Hitler's youth. Arms valiantly held high. The drone of planes filled the air as Churchill's men took up the challenge. 'We'll fight them on the beaches' became our cry as we melted down our pans - and all for what?
A field of poppies?

*Teri Backhouse*

## GREAT AUNT EMILY

About 1920, when I was seven, we were all scared stiff of Dad's great aunt Emily.

Her costume was entirely black, including the vulcanite gums of her false teeth, which were hinged at the back and clacked when she spoke.

Our biggest dread was the farewell 'Dracula Kiss'.

*H Atkinson*

## BEAUTY IN THE POOL

Drink was his downfall. Through it, and what it led to cost him the love of a beautiful woman and his chance of happiness. So forceful was his male vanity and his eccentricity that he faded away to nonentity, leaving in his wake the delicate flower we know as 'Narcissus'.

*Carol Wright*

## ONE ENCHANTED EVENING

They met one lovely evening, introduced by his good friend,
talked and danced, had great fun, then at the evening's end
he took her home, kissed 'goodnight' - they knew it wasn't fate -
for both of them were married, and went home to their mate!
Ah, if only love were all . . .

***Kathleen Adams***

## COMPREHENDING EDUCATION

He met her from the school bus, carried her satchel.
Then looked after the children while she pursued her career.

Kids grown, together again in distant closeness, he often returned inexplicably late. When challenged, he admitted an affair with a bimbo who had time to talk and accompany him fishing.

*K Adlard*

## THE CAGE

She drew nearer the damp, dark cage.
As she drew nearer, the tension mounted.
The sweat on her brow was flooding and pouring.
She was nearly there. The terror was flowing.
Finally, she touched it. 'Ahhh!' she screamed,
'You vicious budgie. I'm not feeding or touching
you again!'

*James Homer (13)*

## IN THE BEGINNING

In the darkness, the relaxing drum beats loud and strong.
I thought it was just a normal day,
that was until the dark broke to light.
I screamed and cried.
I thought this was the end.
But little did I realise, it was only the
beginning, the beginning of life.

*Katie Whittaker (13)*

## THE HAUNTING OF SVEN THE VIKING

Mist fell across the battlefields, as a headless body appeared, wandering, searching. It was Sven the Viking, tragically slain in battle, hunting for his severed head. He found it impaled on a spike. Sven lifted it off, placed it on his shoulders, screamed loud a mighty battle cry, then disappeared.

***Sylvia Bangs***

## FATE OF A FATHER

The man, I cornered, he confessed all. The jungle had seemed carved from emerald. Puffing on his cigar, his forehead broke into perspiration. The alligator had pulled my father into the water by his arm, he said. Someone cried out at the other end of the bar. A glass smashed.

*Ignas Bednarczyk*

## SCHOOL FOR MURDER

They gathered round the body.
'Any thoughts?' queried Inspector Smith.
'Looks like murder sir . . . shot. Probably disturbed a burglar who panicked. But why the scarlet fish?'
'Ignore it,' said Smith, 'It's a red herring.'
The body stirred and rose muttering 'Realistic training's all right, but tomato sauce on my shirt . . . Ugh!'

*Roger Brougham*

## A PUPPET TIED, TO A BLOODIED, LOOPED STRING

Tormented by frenzied voices, screaming out his name;
psychically forcing him to commit horrific violence, at
the surgical slash of a scalpel, across the throats of
writhing, street-walking women. His schizophrenia opening up
his mind to influences from a distant, future readership of
his crimes, as, Jack the Ripper.

*Mark Dunn*

## Narrow Squeak

Now they were near, so near he could hear their voices outside. Keeping low as bullet-holes dotted the walls, how was he going to get out alive?

Then he remembered - the secret passageway!

Quickly he lit his remaining dynamite sticks - before making his escape. Good survived, evil dead.

*C Bond*

## A DAY THAT HE WISHED NEVER WOULD HAVE HAPPENED

My life has changed since that day, I wish that day would go away.
I drove out one day in the car, wasn't looking, wasn't thinking.
I was on the mobile talking to my friend. The child came out of
nowhere. So here I am, hiding at the funeral, ashamed.

*Samantha Heywood*

## CLAN OF FALLON, LIFE ON THE EDGE OF DESPAIR

From Irish famine to Oldham mills,
in drunken brawl breadwinner killed.
Young teenage sons to Scottish mines
and beatings from an uncle, snide.
A champion of Scotland and the oppressed
with twenty offspring one son progressed.
Now grandson can bare his soul
with tales of lust, hate and woe.

*R M Fallon*

## WILLPOWER

Desperately ill, he tossed and turned, his fortune left to his heirs - gamblers all!
He must change the Will! He dragged himself to his office below and, with infinite care, he altered it. Tomorrow it would be witnessed.
Now at peace, he crawled upstairs to bed. He slept and died.

*J Craufurd-Stuart*

## BACK IN ENGLAND BUT WHAT TENSION UNTIL YOU SAW HE WAS IN ONE PIECE

The letter said - Red Cross - in hospital -
do not worry.
Scary - the shades down.
Thank God - it was just his feet.
That certainly was bad enough,
trenchfoot stayed with him always.
Wrote letters for poor
guys with limbs lost.
Little sister read books,
someone noticed they were upside down.
Everyone understood.

*Phyllis O'Connell*

## Rules Are Rules

At last all was ready. The craft was loaded, the cargo safely aboard.
A stillness hung over the port, after the earlier excitement.
The captain rested. Supervision had been intense and tiring.
Suddenly his mate appeared. 'Visitors for you.' 'Who?' he said.
'Folk from the Quarantine Regulation Board.' Noah sighed.

*Alfred Smith*

## Panic

Her first baby has decided to come early.
The phone is dead, it must be the storm.
She is alone, isolated and her car is at the garage.
Tony's late, she panics. The thunder crashes. A car turns in the drive,
it's Tony, he's home, 'Thank God.'

***R Prouse***

## FEAR UNSUBSTANTIATED

'The trees are growing nearer.'
'Rubbish.'
'It's not rubbish. Since you cut down that old oak I've felt afraid.'
'Don't be. It was cracked and dangerous.'
'It was ancient.'
'Precisely. It's time had come.'
That night occurred the worst gale in living memory.
No revengeful trees crashed onto the bungalow.

*Ivy Allpress*

## CHANGING GEAR

Al slid into the bar. A thin guy in a thinner jacket weaved towards the door.
'Take my coat. It's raining outside. Mike's picking me up.'
Befuddled, donning the red, leather coat, Spike lurched into the street. A shot rang out. He fell dead.
Al exited by the rear door.

*Vivien Bayley*

## SWEET VIOLETS

The sombre huddle gazed on the coffin.
Mary stood alone.

'Not from these parts,' whispered mourner;
'That's her niece from Plymouth.'
'Looks deathly; what's that smell?'
'Violets. Ma Palmer loved Dev'n violets.'

Later telegram - *'Mary Bowden killed, A38, coming to Haynes'*
and a sweet smell of violets permeates the room.

**Stephanie Fulfit**

## Two For The Life Of One
## An Autobiography By Dawn Butterfly

Born from pearl-shelled egg, bristling, undulating, self indulgent in greed. My needs, simple, gorging and exploring nettles.
When swollen by gluttony, I surrender to time, to become, to change.
Surrounded by chitinous shroud, waiting, writhing within another soul.
Emerging again, shedding old skin, spreading new wings.
Then flying free.

*Sue Butcher*

## NATURE'S UNNATURAL

The storm broke. The rain came down hard. Its black, matted hair looked strange in the light. The mass of stitches attaching its body together looked unsightly. 'What am I doing?' Frankenstein thought. He looked down at his creation. It was hideous, but it was too late. Lightning had struck.

*Alexa Marsh (15)*

## UNTITLED

World Cup begun, each round was won.
The minutes blinked by, goals anticipated
at every chance. Waiting, painfully.
Breath was held, butterflies flapped furiously.
A sending off, our hearts fell, the closing seconds waiting
for the whistle.
He flew with the ball in dying seconds, a winning goal was scored.

*Adele Lyth*

## The Visit

Huge claws scraped and shook the door.
Beowulf!
Terrified, I reached for the fire stave.
The door crashed open and the hideous creature stood before me.
I thrust the stave into the fire muttering the incantation.
Howling and burning, the monster fled into the night.
I had won - *this* - time.

***Jean Rhodes***

## FUNFAIR

I went on the rides.
This one was fast and scary,
it was 100 feet high,
I wasn't scared,
I think it was fun.
My mum was scared to death,
because she is scared of heights,
so she kept hold of my stepdad,
and when we got off, I felt dizzy.

***Emma Sloan (12)***

## OUR FUTURE

The smog was thick, the oxygen mask uncomfortable. It was normal now. She looked up to a sky where songbirds once flew. She felt guilty, but how was she to know? Who thought that a bit of pollution would result in this? We can't blame ourselves she said.

***Emma Norris (16)***

## A Seven-Year-Old's Tale Of Terror

Like a hunted animal, Lizzie sat tensed, every instinct telling her to flee. But, trapped, all she could do was watch in horror as the masked man approached. Seconds later, she blacked out.

It could have been worse, she told herself later, feeling the gap with her tongue. No problem.

*Julia Roe (16)*

## ALL IS VANITY

She winked at him all through the train journey. He was flattered.
A young girl and a man of sixty five. Perfect bliss!
On the station he made a pass, and she slapped his face.
He was confused! Then he understood! As pretty as she was,
she had a nervous tick.

*Joyce Brannelly*

# SOMETIMES, AS WE LOOK FORWARD, FATE PLAYS A CRUEL TRICK

As she sat by the window watching the countryside flash by, Mary thought of Jim. She had been right to end it, he was unfaithful, but it hurt. She took stock. She was young, free, everything ahead of her. Suddenly there was a sickening lurch. Mary screamed - then silent blackness.

*Wendy Ray*

## THE SEA CAN BE CRUEL AND UNRELENTING YET THE URGE TO CONQUER IS EVER PRESENT

Sail around the world, that was Peter's dream, it became a harsh reality.
So many attempts by others, his first too, was thwarted.
Bedraggled but triumphant return with glowing success.
Content now to watch others succeed and fail, knowing the reasons why.

*Mary Gardner*

# THE STONE

They heaved the stone they saw as evil from their lives and left it to the ravages of weather's grip. But in another age, men took the stone and carved it to an image of their gods and waged the war that laid an empire wasted for a thousand years.

*Brian Parvin*

## WHO NEEDS ENEMIES?

After colonising that damp, misty island and conquering Gaul, it was good to be home.

At the Forum, Cassius and the others stood apart and I wondered why. Suddenly I felt a sharp pain, turned and saw my friend, his dagger dripping blood. 'Why you Brutus?' were my dying words.

*Cynthia C Berry*

## THE DRAMA SAGA, OR, IT SEEMED LIKE A GOOD IDEA TO START A DRAMA GROUP

'Interested in amateur dramatics?' adverts resulted in a first meeting of like-minded souls, and some enjoyable evenings of improvisation etc. followed.

But, although we thought we knew what we wanted to do, we couldn't agree on how.

Less than six months and two extra-marital affairs later, we folded.

*J Brookes*

## BOX TUNNEL

It was a feat of engineering genius. He thought and planned and many people slaved in an effort to make his dream come true. He knew it could work. They dug and sweated until at last they achieved success. Brunel could see the light at the end of the tunnel.

*Sallie Chilcott*

## MY ONE AND ONLY SOULMATE

The sorrow of the goodbye was heartbreaking as the train slowly went by. I knew I would never see him again, so all I could do was cry, my life felt as though it was fading away. I needed him, for he was my soulmate, the one I could trust.

*Kerry Ward (15)*

## THE STATUETTE

On holiday I bought a mysterious statuette.
As time went on, bad things happened around me.
Was it the statuette or superstition?
I gave it away to the jumble. Free!
Later, tragedy, my friend died in an accident
on her way home from the jumble.
Guess what I received in her will . . . ?

***Sharon Walker (15)***

## SHE WATCHED THE RIDES GO AROUND AS HE ASKED HER INTO THE HALL OF MIRRORS

Kate was laughing at her hilarious reflections in the mirror. First she was fat and then she was thin.

Kate turned to see the man's reflection, but he had disappeared.
The room closed in. There was no escape.
She couldn't breathe. Would she ever get out?
Then Kate suddenly awoke.

*Claire Hancock (15)*

## PAINFUL ENCOUNTER

Fingers clasped white together, hands entwine. Eyes fall into his, sweat falls from my brow. Lips pursed then open to release a scream that won't leave my tongue. His frown deepens, hands clasp tighter, the grip cuts off the circulation. *'Peanuts!'* Clasp released, my fingers bent beyond recognition! He won!

***Vicky Purnell (15)***

## ON THE FLOOR

Everything glimmered and shone as she approached. His once black and white life lit up as the technicolour of her beauty touched him. She sat down opposite him and looked into his eyes. A smile started to spread over her face,
'No! No!' yelled the director, 'You're doing it again!'

*William Law (15)*

## TIME TRAVEL

The dark figure approached him out of the shadowy gloom. He felt totally alone on the bridge. There seemed no escape but to jump. So this he did, and fell through the blackness to oblivion, hearing faint words from above saying 'Dearie me - I only wanted to know the time!'

*D Falck*

## 'REMEMBER WHEN . . . ?'

Children's voices, happy innocence of youth. Young men's lust, pretty girls, hurried fumblings of inexperienced fingers . . . making love. Off to war, brave young men to die. Shell-shocked; wounded; home again. Pretty girls and youth all gone . . . long, empty life ahead. Memories return and an old man smiles again.

***Joanne Burns***

## THE STUFF DREAMS ARE MADE FROM

One hundred thousand football fans cheered both sides onto the pitch. The British manager knew he was on the edge of greatness as the first coach to achieve a unique treble in one season.
The Cup Final
The Premiership
Tonight, the European Champion's Cup?
Just one more team to beat.

***A Doubler***

## DISTOPIA IN 50 WORDS AND A NUMBER

It was his weekly check at the Ministry of Health, but he was worried something was wrong.
'Enter 2014' the machine voice barked. He climbed into the chair he knew so well.
The computer scanned him and beeped.
He knew he must leave, then a sharp pain, and he was gone.

***Kay Reynoldson (13)***

## HOLIDAY NIGHTMARE

James was very excited he was going on holiday.
His parents told him he was going to Spain.
He was thirteen and that's when most boys first
go on holiday on their own.
When he arrived in Spain, a skinny boy greeted him,
'Welcome to the island where you'll die.'

*Daniel Pillar (13)*

## A Miracle Is An Unexpected Blessing

He planned to work here for just five years. As they flew over the island she fell in love with it. Stepping out of the plane she felt at home. Back in England she heard she had been left a house so now, a widow, Jersey is really her home.

*Mabel Helen Underwood*

## Burglar

I lie in bed. I hear a noise. Someone is in the house. My heart beats fast. Out of bed I jump. A clatter is heard. What shall I do? Looking for something hard. Cannot find anything. Creeping downstairs I see Mum and Dad returning from holiday early.

*Jenny Bosworth*

## ANOTHER NIGHT ALONE, BUT NOT ALONE

The wind is howling and whistling outside, only my fire to keep me warm and give me light. As I sit inside my tiny hut, my door is locked to protect me from terror that may come, and hurt. But in God I put my trust.

*Sandra Rose*

## TILL DEATH DO US PART

Two graves, not one; far away from each other.
Lucy's heart ached with memories of her happy and loving parents' constant promises that 'We'll always be together'.
Now, after their tragic death, she brushed away angry tears as she laid her flowers.
'Oh, why did you never marry?' she sobbed.

*Elsa Wilson*

## JACK'S MYSTERIOUS BIRTHDAY

It's Jack's birthday and he's going on an aeroplane -
but it's more like a spaceship.
He boarded the ship. He got taken to two conveyor belts.
The strange people stuck him on the conveyor belt, and
down slowly he went, and at the very end, aliens stood waiting for tea.

*Adrian Colley (13)*

## THE INTRUDER

Nothing would ever be the same again. The lone figure, which had slipped in among them, had changed everything. One minute, things were as they had been for years before. The next, the arrival of this single figure had made all the difference. Yes, The Millennium had come at last!

*Heather Henry*

## I'll Show You, Billy Boy!

Cruelly dumping poor Doreen from the post-room, Billy set his sights on Muriel Arbuthnot, his chairman's daughter. Marital misery ensued. Billy returned to sorting post. And Doreen? Well, she and old Arbuthnot spent ecstatic nights in Nice just before his rapturous finale in their honeymoon bed. She inherited the lot!

*Sylvia Bray*

## THE UNSEEN ENEMY

Obeying orders he buried the thing, then he and the war moved on.
Years later, aged ten, black, full of fun, loving to jump and run - he stepped on the thing.
His leg, his youth and his future, all gone - but the war he had never known had come back.

*George Woodham*

## THE ASCENT - OCTOBER 1870

Horatio climbed upwards through the blackness. Heart pounding, he slowly, inexorably clawed his way towards the summit he'd begun to despair of reaching. So many depending on him . . . one last effort . . . Suddenly, daylight flooded in on him, as the juvenile sweep finally forced his brush free of the chimney pot.

*Alan Titley*

## THE CELEBRATION

He would ask her tonight, Jessica felt sure. She gazed softly across the table at him, their eyes met mid candlelight. Tom's large hand clasped hers, his brown eyes brimmed with hope. 'Well Jess, will you?' She smiled and raised her glass. 'Yes brother dear, I'll join the family firm!'

*Linda Jefferies*

## TO HAVE AND TO HOLD

He looked, a question in his eyes.
She answered smiling.
They sat in the chapel in wheelchairs.
The priest stumbled slightly over the worlds 'Till death us do part.'
Their responses came out strongly.
They went back to the ward, hand in hand, to the hell of chemotherapy,
Heaven in their hearts.

*J Gray*

## A SPIDER'S SHORT LIFE

There was blood dripping from an open wound on her father's face, but Sarah couldn't help staring at the spider that was crawling towards it. Like a swimmer preparing to dive into a pool, the spider's black legs edged closer to the gash. Sarah's mother walked in and smacked the spider clean off the drunk's face.

*D Croasdell*

## MARATHON MAN - THE ULTIMATE CHALLENGE TO REACH THE FINISH

Mile after mile, never ending strides. With unbearable pain, the sweat rolls down, but victory must be delivered to the crowds. He reaches the finish and the message of victory is out. The crowds roar, the pain is finally over, as he falls to the ground. The Persians have lost.

*Ella Pearson (14)*

## THINGS THAT GO BUMP IN THE NIGHT!
## (IF YOU'RE A STALKER, SILENCE IS THE KEY!)

The girl crept slowly down the corridor to where he lay sleeping. She edged nearer, determined not to wake him. She reached for the door and pulled. With a screech it opened, and he woke! With an angry cry, her hamster launched himself across the cage and bit her finger.

*Amy Law (14)*

## NEW TERM, NEW SUBJECT, THIS TERM IT'S...

'School' Mum shouted upstairs.
I got out of bed and went downstairs,
'Do I have to go today?'
'Yes!' Mum persisted.
I had breakfast then left for school.
First lesson went fine, but second was PE.
The teacher bawled 'New term, new subject,
this term it's . . . *Russian Roulette* . . . you're first!'

**Richard Farren (12)**

## DESMOND'S AS LIGHT AS A FEATHER

Desmond didn't know why his parents were taking him. Britain was ruled by Hopkin, he ordered that nobody was allowed to have exercise and had to be a set weight, he was insanely overweight. Desmond was going to be weighed. He was underweight and was therefore given an execution.

*Adam Gardner (13)*

## EXPLOSION

The bomb was set to explode at midnight. James had fallen, his leg was broken. He crawled to the door, five minutes to midnight. He had to get out - the lock wouldn't move. Ironical! James was trying to blow up his rival.

*Marcella DeSantis*

## A Living Hell

Midday sun. Blistering heat and unbearable loneliness. The Strontium Desert Expedition had gone horribly wrong. No one had listened - the entire team of scientists and troopers, save one man, had perished from drinking polluted water.

Now McStevens, withered from extreme exhaustion, stumbles towards base camp - raw anger fuelling his desire to live.

*Angus Brown*

## ON THE TRAIN

Through the crowded carriage she spied him. He was reading the Telegraph. How predictable. She stared hard, willing him to see her: a briefcase now, not a paperback on the beach. Ibiza, did he remember? A child behind her began to scream, he looked up, irritated. Their eyes met. Nothing.

*Vivienne Buckley*

## THE LADY

What of the lady of the lake for many a tale has been told
of this fable the lonely figure of her and the sword Excalibur
twas the gift she gave to Merlin
it was made when lightning hit the water

***Jonathon Covington***

## SOAKING UP THE SUN ON BIKINI ATOLL

We should have worn sunglasses - *wow* the sky was bright that day: the world's biggest explosion.

The Japanese didn't see it coming either, thousands killed in seconds.

We were looking for world peace - never to be though - I never did see anything else after that day. Should have worn sunglasses . . .

**Pat Derbyshire**

## WERE WE DINNER?

We were taken into a ship, being told that
we would have more fun than ever.
It was dark and wet and then a voice,
'Keep to the left and walk forwards.'
We walked into a room full of
plates and glasses, they were empty,
but why?
Were we dinner?

*Holly Langdale (12)*

## The Alien World!

We were on a grey planet. I looked around. There were these . . . aliens. Ten of them took us into a cold room. There was this box which said 'Parts' on it. A 'Doctor' then took me away. He pointed to a table. I lay down . . . and heard a cutting noise!

*Felicity Gibbeson (13)*

## 2034

It was July 2034. A special TV news report was about to start. The phone rang, grandma said, 'I'm coming round now.' The doorbell rang. Dad answered it. *'Aaarrgghh'* he yelled. The newsreader was saying 'Robots have malfunctioned, don't open your doors!' Mum and I said in unison, *'Too late!'*

**James Murray (13)**

## TALENT

He stood on the corner of the mat, silent as eyes stared at him . . . waiting. He leaped forwards and somersaulted into the air, twisting and turning. He landed on his feet perfectly; a smile rose to his face as the audience applauded and cheered.
Larry indeed was no ordinary frog.

**Thomas Wignall (15)**

## A Personal Story

It seemed impossible that he could leave her. They had been so close, inseparable for many months. The pain. The tears - not just hers. She felt she was responsible for pushing him away.
'You have a beautiful boy,' the midwife told her.

***Bryony Hutchinson***

## PURSUIT

His feet pounded over the dry leaves,
a trickle of sweat ran into his eye.
He checked behind him.
A choked sob escaped from his mouth,
his pursuer was gaining on him.
He cried with relief as he crossed the finish line.

*Jonathan Wadsworth (12)*

## THE POLYCHROME PROMISE

How it had rained!

For days, a hundred sad eyes gazed
upwards and a slate sky stared back.

Skies wept - eyes slept.

An eternity passed . . .

One day, a multicoloured ribbon
swathed the blue-again sky.

Eyes gleamed joyfully and, lost
in beauty, none noticed Noah
shed a silent, grateful tear . . .

***Susan Devlin***

## STALKED - THE STORY OF MENTAL TORTURE THAT NO PUNISHMENT CAN ERASE

'Guilty,' announced the foreman.
'It's all over love,' whispered Dan. 'He can't touch you anymore.'
All eyes were on me; only his penetrated my soul.
For two hellish years he lurked; following my every waking move.
They removed him from court in seconds.
Years later the nightmare still won't fade.

*Helen Bancroft*

## TWELVE MORE BLACKED-OUT MILES TO 23.59 AT CAMP!

*Bbbrrrmm* . . . 'A buzzbomb!' The flame was overhead as she pedalled furiously towards the turn: the crash and a *'moo'* told all.
'Cor, you look like a ghost!' Dot falsified the time by five minutes . . .
'I nearly became one!' gasped Margaret.

***Margaret Clary***

## CHOOSING THE FUTURE

He had everything. A beautiful wife and a beautiful home. They wanted for nothing. Problems had never been encountered. Yet he had been told that he was missing something. He had never looked for more, but the temptation now proved too great. Yes or no!

Eve handed him the apple.

***Charlotte Clark***

# A Shiny K-night

In days of honour,
chivalrous knights scour the kingdom
for the evil dragon foe.
With clinking of swords,
a roar and a thunderous flame.
The aftermath, head of the prize
hauled back for a victory claim.
Calmly returning to the stone-built tower,
proving to the damsel 'all is well'.

*Paul Warwick*

## MYSTERIOUS ABDUCTION

Forty years in the future, aliens landed on earth. We were taken to another world. People were lined up outside a large building, not knowing what to expect. I went into a plain room; came out of the room and sat next to a man. He looked exactly like me.

*James Peacock (12)*

## SHOPPING CAN BE DANGEROUS!

*'Aaaaaarrrrgggghhh!'* Sophie stepped into the shop and towards the giant, hairy crocodile, eating CDs. People yelled at her to run, but instead she steadily advanced. The brute's eyes softened and she sauntered right up to it. One gulp and she disappeared. You thought it would be a happy ending, didn't you?

**Chris Jones (12)**

## THE CAN SURPRISE

I was walking down the street and I went into the usual shop. It was a newsagent's. I picked up a can. It felt quite light, the shopkeeper thought so too. I paid for it and went outside. I started opening it and to my surprise, it was totally *empty!*

**Martin Karetnyk (12)**

## FATAL ASTHMA

Government experiment for the eradication of asthma, room 501, 21st June. I was excited because my asthma was being cured. Dad drove me to a large building. Inside a small room I was injected with some formula. At home the phone rang, 'Would you like your daughter buried or frozen?'

*Claire Parkinson (13)*

# EASY STREET?

James Royle wore a smug smile as he left the bank.
'Easy Street here I come!' His million was safe.
Three hours to kill - time for a show and a few beers.
He was tipping the waitress when the shooting started.
Goodbye, James Royle of Easy Street and easier virtue.

***Betty Lightfoot***

## A CLOSE SAVE

As the words filtered through to the blank expression, a soft tapping could be heard. Slowly the meaning became very clear to the all seeing eye. At this moment a sardonic smile broke out on the face of Millennia as the words before her read the 'Millennium Bug is dead.'

*Jean Anderson Fowler*

## AS IT IS ON EARTH, SO IT SHALL BE IN HEAVEN

Ronwald had died,
Christina slept on his grave heartbroken.
Suddenly she heard his voice saying 'Do not
worry, soon we shall be together.'
Cold and wet, fever struck and she had a
vision. Ronwald was dressed in white, waiting
for her.
A white dove appeared, closing her eyes she smiled.

*B J Harrison*

## THE MYSTERY OF THE EAST POLE

No one had thought it was possible;
No one believed it was there;
*But it was!*
Buried beneath the sands of time
Close to Cromer Pier;
Signs of the first attempt to find the
most easterly point in this land:
All that remained was -
Pith helmet and an umbrella stand.

*Michael Childs*

## MODERN ARK

A blistering *c-r-a-c-k* separated the sky like permanent lightning as the ultibomb exploded.
The sea evaporated.
Resembling a decapitated egg, half the world careered wildly away skywards. The other half shuddered in its crozzled shell and Noah the Second's knowing smile froze as his indestructible animal shelter started to melt.

***E P Jones***

## UNTITLED

'Dear get down here now. You have
to go to school.'
'But I don't want to
go all the children pick on me and call
me names they say I am fat. I don't
like it.'
'But you have to.'
'No I don't.'
'Yes you do you are the
*Headmaster!*'

***Amanda Couch (12)***

## THE CONCERT!

'You're on in 2 minutes,' said the floor manager.
The band were just about to go on stage. The screen on the stage said *'Are you ready for showtime!'*
Rebecca and Jo were screaming and shouting, then a loud blast of music, 3 minutes 45 seconds later the CD player finished.

**Charlotte McNiven (12)**

## GRANDMA'S FUNERAL

'But why must it be Gran?'
asked Janie.
'It was going to happen someday,
it just happened to be today,'
answered Mum, 'Grandma will
be looked after in heaven!'
'I suppose so,' said Janie sobbing,
'When's the funeral?'
Mum replied, 'Well, I think
we'd better carry out the
murder first!'

**Katy Scott-Nelson (13)**

## MY VISIT TO THE HOSPITAL

It was a bright early morning.
Today I was going to the
hospital for a leg operation.
I was placed on a large bed,
then the doctor injected me
and I slowly dosed off.
When I woke up little did I know
I had been cloned.

*Katie Jameson (13)*

## 2023

Starving people were scattered
along the streets, mobbing
anyone who had a scrap of food.
A government car cruised by,
someone inside shouted,
'I've got food!' We followed.
Food at last!
We were directed to a room with
a table full of food. I took a bite,
swayed violently, and collapsed.

*Joanne Lax (13)*

## THE CREATOR OF THE JOKE KNEW; DINOSAURS NEVER LAUGHED, THEY HAD NO FAITH IN JOKES

A joke began it.
Everyone started to smile.
Presidents, politicians, policemen,
pop stars, protesters, populations.
Smiles turned to laughter.
Laughter became hysterical.
Many died of paroxysms.
Philosophers aware of the joke, found it frustrating
that a species should die, unaware of the joker.

*Richard Cluroe*

## ODIN'S CHILDREN

Odin reigned, Viking sailors, shipwrecked, settled in Celtic Wales, scoured fields and left me their name - Scourfield. Now I have seen Norway, met Norsemen, heard legends of mountains and fjords, felt my ancestry. Widowed mother of four tall, redheaded, grown-up children, fulfilled my dreams, maybe Odin's children live on.

*Frieda Cox*

## PIPPED AT THE POST

Jenny had left the secretarial post six months ago.
She was meeting Sara and Emma at the restaurant.
 'I've divorced Charles,' declared Sara sipping coffee.
 'Simon Fellow's my type, very wealthy.'
 'But I'm his personal secretary,' purred Emma.
 'And I married him six months ago,' grinned Jenny,
 'more coffee anyone?'

*M Williams*

## UNTITLED

Tension was not why I signed up, but I always knew it to be a risk, and now, one on one we had completed our initial exchanges. The object flew towards my skull. Decision time. Okay, hook it, the ashes will be ours.

*Susan Hurst (14)*

## WHAT IF IT ALL WENT WRONG?

She entered the room and sat down. She tried to reassure herself that she had done all she could, that it would be all over soon, but the panic worsened. What if it all went wrong? She took a deep breath and said, 'You may open your exam papers now.'

***Charlotte Barlow (14)***

## HEAVEN IS . . .?

Janet couldn't believe her luck, sitting in the tea shop surrounded by scrumptious cakes.

'I'm in heaven,' she smirked as she tucked in greedily. Failed diets and tantrums were now history.

The more Janet ate, more goodies appeared - more and more cakes . . . an endless supply, an eternal supply of cakes . . .

*Pamela Taylor Marshall*

## THE MEETING

They would have said I was mad if they had known. Maybe I was!
I could hardly see out of the car, but he was there. He smiled. It was fate!
There were no secrets when we met at Gretna. Everyone was there and the sun was shining!

*Angela Robinson*

## LET THERE BE RAIN

The world was like a mouldy apple - rotten to the core. A decision was made to destroy every living creature, but God was merciful. Noah built the first Titanic, setting sail with two of every animal. After 960 hours, the rain stopped. Noah wasn't wet. The earth was very clean.

*Claire Harrison (13)*

## Dusk Encounter

He was a defiant sceptic.
Yet as dusk enveloped the Loch,
the raft felt small and vulnerable.
Shivering, the myth of Ness whispered
deep into his senses.
Breathlessly he examined the water's murky
surface, looming large beneath him.
Suddenly he knew he was not alone.
No-one ever heard his scream.

***Tim Belton***

## Untitled

Everyone said the shining wire ring was special. 'If you go into it, you'll go somewhere far away,' they all told him - some did and they never came back, so they must be happy he thought. He had expected it to be pleasant, the snare tightened around the rabbit's neck.

***Catherine Spurden (13)***

## Untitled

He was falling from the clouds, blue sky all around him. The wind blowing in his face as he fell. The earth looked far away. He came to the ground with a thud. 'Well done, you have achieved parachuting.'

*Natalie Jeffery (14)*

## HOW LORD RUSSELL DE WARE MET HIS LADY

Lord Russel was competing at the Lists one day, when he was summoned to his brother's, Lord John, whose castle was being attacked, they arrived in time to win the day.
At night there was feasting and dancing, and that's where Lord Russel met his lady, the beautiful Lady Elenore.

***Yvonne E Hicks***

## WHO CAN FORETELL WHAT LURKS MALEVOLENTLY ON A BEAUTIFUL QUIET BEACH ON A SUMMER'S MORN?

Sharp bang, Maud halted, calm sea, she saw it, a huge black pot, protruding horns, hitting the rocks, she knew, a sea mine waiting to explode, run run, face down into bushes.
An explosion, blood trickling down her leg, pieces raining down everywhere.
Calm, escape, a transformed seashore. Shock.

*Brigid O'Donnell*

## LONELY NIGHTS

I'm all alone, I'm scared, is he feeling the same as me? I mean is our love strong enough to survive. Or is it the end, is our love going to die. I can't handle the emotion, I need him with me, by my side. Come back, I miss you.

**Michelle Barnes**

## A Silver Wedding Anniversary

A young couple spent honeymoon at aunt's seaside house. Afraid of offending her, they limited their love making. Twenty-five years later same couple on second honeymoon had romance spoilt by noisy hotel. Made love in a car and were stopped by a policeman, who didn't believe they were married.

*Joan G Brown*

## MY MATE HAD WARNED ME
## HE HAD NEIGHBOURS FROM HELL . . .

. . . Rave-up party.
Then this huge gate-crasher mangled a guest.
I grabbed him - but he ran off, leaving his arm behind. He dripped blood to the poolside. I dived after him.
Grendel's last words were:
'My mum's bigger than yours, Beowulf!'
She was, too. I spun round to face her . . .
Scary.

*Chris Creedon*

## JECOLVIC'S FEAR

From the time of the Vikings the Andersson family were in fear of being murdered. Jecolvic was the last one to be alive he was terrified. His cabin was secure and weatherproof yet he felt alarmed, he was being watched! The wind screeched the fire roared, Jecolvic was throttled!

*Alma Montgomery Frank*

## MERSEYSIDE - DECEMBER, 1940

Sirens wailed, searchlights swept the sky and ack-ack clattered. Bombers droned overhead and bombs screamed down. The fences blazed. As sand extinguished them, the kitchen imploded. Glass, water and soot covered everywhere. Dawn eventually broke and another night had been survived. Board up the windows and go to work!

*J Robinson*

## THE INTERVIEW

He walked out of the room and sighed with relief, at last the interview had ended. It was his first time doing it and he was nervous. He had asked different people how to set it out. Now all he needed was to find the person suitable for the job.

***Charlena Rooney (14)***

## IT WAS FIFTY YEARS AGO TODAY - DOLLY WAS THIRTY-FIVE YEARS OLD

After waiting three hours for her hospital appointment, Dolly was seen by a sombre, grey-haired doctor and given four weeks to live.
Dolly returned home devastated.
Next morning there was a knock at the door. Results had been confused, Dolly was clear.
She accepted all apologies - life went on.

*Dorothy Whitehall*

## JACKPOT

'Tonight's machine is Guinevere, set of balls 6.'
James sat holding the pink ticket.
'And the first ball is number 8.'
'Yes,' yelled James, '2 more to go.'
'Ball number 2 is 12.'
'1 more ball and I'm rich.'
'Ball number 3 is . . . 29.'
Jack looked at the TV with stunned eyes.
'Another game, another loss' he shouted!

**Laura Baudoino (12)**

## THE VAGRANT

They called him a vagrant. I remember his days of a salesman, times were good, family were there, money never short.
Changed days were facing him, little did he know. Wife died, children went their ways. He took to drink and downwards he went. Cardboard City he now stays.

*Pat Trixie Ashcroft*

## WHAT SIGHTS

What sights awaited him Icarus thought, a week in space to see it all, and then a lifetime to talk about it all to people who would never get tired of it all. Looking around for a week before going home again is very easy, or so Icarus thought . . .

***Keith L Powell***

## THE JOURNEY TO HULL

Brum, brum. 'Look' said Andrew 'it's the mini bus.'
'Jump in' said the driver. On the way Andrew sang
'We're going skating!' The rest were annoyed at Andrew.
Dean turned round and said 'Oh shut up you!' The driver said
'We're here' and Andrew saw we were at Laser Quest.

*Thomas Woodcock (12)*

## BADMINTON

Fourteen, all match point, my serve.
It had been a very tough, hard,
tiring game. Nevertheless I still
enjoyed every minute of it. This was
the biggest game of the season.
I served, he cleared back to me.
'Smash' the crowd were going
wild. I had won the game.

*Luke Alker (12)*

## CASSANDRA THE SORCERESS WAS EXPELLED AS A FAILURE. NONE OF HER SPELLS HAD EVER WORKED

Her last assignment had been sticking pins into dolls resembling people. This had not been successful. Reluctantly she cleared out her belongings, dumped her rubbish in the incinerator and left. Police were completely baffled as thirty people were found dead. All had been burned although none were near fire!

*Anna Bruce Hausrath*

## SSH! A NOISE?

A cry was heard below the floorboards.
Creaking, the wooden plank lifted.
Glistening the darkest corner was two sharp beaded eyes.
A helping hand lowered towards the creature,
still crying the terrified bawl became fur.
Lifted out slowly its appearance was known as a weak starved kitten.

**Heather Edwards**

## THE LAST LAUGH OF ELLASAR WHOSE NAME MEANS REVOLTING FROM GOD

The homeward climb had left Ellasar breathless, but he chuckled thinking of how he would enjoy telling about the man who had built a wooden monstrosity because he believed water would soon cover the mountains. Laughing Ellasar watched the speck of wood far below, until his eyes overflowed with water.

*Maida E Barclay*

## ARCHIMEDES?

He lay contentedly soaking in the warm bath water until suddenly leaping out dripping everywhere and crying Eureka! A great discovery? - A famous man?- No, the anonymous voice from the radio had just announced to Joe Bloggs that his numbers were up, all six in fact on the midweek lottery!

*Linda Rowley*

## 50-WORD STORY

Zane walked along the beach, the cool breeze rippling through his black, spiky hair, the sound of Offspring pumping through his headphones. Suddenly Corrie ran towards him, she ran fastly against the wind. Zane ran towards her. Corrie stopped running.
'What's wrong Corrie?'
Zane said anxiously to his old, beloved dog.

***Sharice Barkhordarian (12)***

## THE PAST RETRIEVED

Their honeymoon house - now derelict.
She sighed, instinctively reaching under the flowerpot for a key.
There was no key but she produced a ring. Careful cleaning revealed a gold wedding ring and there was an inscription - 'Myra and Josh. 23.6.68'
It was her original wedding ring, lost thirty years ago.

*Pauline Phillips*

## THE GREAT RACE

Lee was riding Sultan, they were at the 19th fence in the Grand National, the sky was blue and there was only 13 horses left. They were coming up to the last fence, it looked like a clear jump but Sultan fell, Lee sat down and Sultan kept on running.

***Catherine Sucksmith (12)***

## THE WRONG VAN

Hello, I am Deano. One day I went to see my friend. I asked him if he wanted to go to the Project Van. He said, 'Okay.' We went down and joined Martin. It wasn't the usual van. A person then walked by and said, 'Get out of that ambulance!'

*David Dean (12)*

## WALKING SIXTEEN MILES AT
## NIGHT THROUGH THE BLITZ...

Tired. They marched in army boots.
A precarious sky shook and flamed and rattled.
At dawn, they found a bakery
where sunrise coloured a rural sky.
They ate warm bread and drank hot cocoa,
then slept on sacks of flour,
and forgot for a while, about going back.

**Susan Roberts**

## BANDITO'S LOVE

The brave parrot Bandito dreamed of his home, Uangitoto, of the palms and flowers and his free native skies.

His heart quivered as he saw the sparrow fly. Little Mary found him on the cage floor, but he was already soaring in a better place, where he found his mate.

*Christina Martin*

## A 20TH CENTURY LOVE STORY

I simply must get to the house-party this weekend.
I've had my mind made up to meet the guest of honour ever since I came to England.
Now I'm sniffing and croaking with an awful cold; he'll never notice me.
That evening: 'Your Royal Highness, may I introduce Mrs Simpson.'

*Margaret Carl Hibbs*

## FACE TO FACE

Veronique had to face the face she'd hated. The face-off was inevitable, but face it she must or lose face. With no time for an about face, she turned sharply and faced the unknown face in her mirror, then smiled. She was face to face with a beautiful facelift.

*Tony Woods-McLean*

## MILLENNIUM

They sent him on a journey
of a thousand years
from a godless planet dying.
Deep frozen and without dream
they wrapped him in tin foil,
to faithfully preserve
the last of a forgotten line.
Yet near Andromeda
in his deep loneliness,
his starship faltered
and something stirred
      - and touched him.

*Norman Royal*

## OUT OF CONTROL

The original feeling had been fantastic. An almighty high like nothing ever felt before. Amazing that one tiny capsule could do so much.
Then things began to go wrong. Fighting for breath, sweating, terrified. Muffled voices and blurred faces as the blackness took over.
Sam remembered the warnings too late.

*Gillian Snaith*

## AUGUST THE THIRTIETH, NINETEEN SEVENTY FOUR

Friday morning, it rained, but nothing could dampen her spirits on this special day.
At the registry office, she joined her partner for their wedding service. She was dressed in white wedding attire, him in best suit.
Eventually, the sun shone, enabling several photographs to be taken, providing everlasting memories.

*S Mullinger*

## THE DEAD BODY

'I'm going out,' said Bob.
'OK,' said his mum.
When Bob got outside he got the
shock of his life. Terry was waiting.
They went round the back to play football.
The ball went into the bin. There was
a body there.
'Don't worry,' said Bob, 'it's only a doll!'

*Neil Fraser (12)*

## FAMILY LIFE

'Come down here now!' Hannah shouted.
'What do you want now?' Jack grumbled.
'Have you tidied up your room yet?' asked Hannah.
'No!' Jack shouted back.
'Hurry up then, your programme is on now,' called Hannah.
'So what is for tea?' asked Jack.
'It is our wedding anniversary soon Jack.'

**Tom Blair (12)**

## C AND WHY

Youthful dreamer wartime fireman shovelling coal,
blown up sewn up back to work as a chemic', filled
his pipe and puffed on.
Fished the trout into retirement, cared for his garden,
tied flies.
Cancer they told him, of the lungs -
I'll fight it like a salmon.
Scattered his ashes yesterday.

*Roger W Chamberlain*

## SOME STATUES LAST FOREVER, BUT FORGET WHAT PURPOSE THEY SERVE

She sped across the ocean,
a gift from France.
And found herself with
her own island, realising the huddled masses
were calling her hope. But the weight
on her shoulders was great, the expectation too
high, so she turned her head and blew out that torch,
her touch of Liberty.

*Anthony Lascelle*

## SILVER AND BLUE

A silver throated cat
sat down next to me
he looked me up and down
stared at me
as if to say
I'm magical, look at me
the mystery in his deep blue eyes
terrified my soul
so I spread my wings
and flew away
before he could eat me.

***J M Stoles***

## DEATH OF THE AMERICAN DREAM

He tested the rifle for balance.
Squinting along the barrel, he swayed gently
From side to side.
Satisfied, he waited . . .
        An hour later, the rifle nestling
In his shoulder, he adjusted the sight.
With his victim's head in sharp focus in the cross hairs,
Lee Harvey Oswald pulled the trigger . . .

***Keith Tissington***

## A Packet Of Fags

'A packet of Mayfair fags please.'
'How old are you please?'
'I'm 17 sir, can I have a lighter as well sir.'
'Do you want a fag Gemma.'
'Yes go on then.'
'And what are you doing lady,' said her mum
'You can come home and eat the fags, you're 14.'

**Barry Flory (12)**

## £5000

Richard sat down and started to watch the TV. On the screen it said, if you ring this number you will win £5000 if you get through first. Richard rang the number. 'Hello' someone said. 'Yes I've won £5000 I got through.' 'You have the wrong number.' Oh no.

*Fiona Wainwright (11)*

## WHILST TAKING MY MORNING STROLL ON MY FAVOURITE DESERTED BEACH I HAD A STRANGE ENCOUNTER

I opened my eyes to a Viking rising up
from the early morning mist.
In his hand he held an upturned helmet.
Walking towards me; with arms out-
stretched; indicating me to drink.
I sipped the sweet liquid.
Looking up, he had melted into the mist;
leaving only his helmet behind.

*Janet Rimmer*

## ON THE STEPS OF THE CHURCH

She wasn't sure she wanted this but mother insisted she try. Later, if she wasn't happy she could leave. Would anything change her mind? Dressed all in white she heard the music and was inspired. She moved confidently now and walked towards the altar, the novice nun, her doubts gone.

*Channon Cornwallis*

# SUBMISSIONS INVITED
## *SOMETHING FOR EVERYONE*

**ANCHOR BOOKS '99** - Any subject, light-hearted clean fun, nothing unprintable please.

**WOMENSWORDS '99** - Strictly women, have your say the female way!

**STRONGWORDS '99** - Warning! Age restriction, must be between 16-24, opinionated and have strong views. (Not for the faint-hearted)

All poems no longer than 30 lines.
Always welcome! No fee!
Cash Prizes to be won!

Mark your envelope (eg *Poetry Now)* **'99**
Send to:
Forward Press Ltd
Remus House, Coltsfoot Drive
Woodston
Peterborough, PE2 9JX

**OVER £10,000 POETRY PRIZES TO BE WON!**
Judging will take place in October 1999